Snowy day

Mick Manning and
Brita Granström

W

FRANKLIN WATTS
NEW YORK • LONDON • SYDNEY

It had been cold for days.
Then it started to snow.

It snowed all night and I dreamed about polar bears and penguins.

In the morning the sky was
a whirl of snowflakes.

After lunch we made a snowman
and gave it my Dad's old hat.

We sledged through the park until it was time to go home.

The snow sounded scrunchy under our wellies.

We were having our tea.
There was a knock on
the door...

I opened it and there was my snowman!

I hid behind Mum,
but she just laughed.

It was my Dad all covered in snow!

Sharing books with your child

Early Worms are a range of books for you to share with your child. Together you can look at the pictures and talk about the subject or story. Listening, looking and talking are the first vital stages in children's reading development, and lay the early foundation for good reading habits.

Talking about the pictures is the first step in involving children in the pages of a book, especially if the subject or story can be related to their own familiar world. When children can relate the matter in the book to their own experience, this can be used as a starting point for introducing new knowledge, whether it is counting, getting to know colours or finding out how other people live.

Gradually children will develop their listening and concentration skills as well as a sense of what a book is. Soon they will learn how a book works: that you turn the pages from right to left, and read the story from left to right on a double page. They start to realize that the black marks on the page have a meaning and that they relate to the pictures. Once children have grasped these basic essentials they will develop strategies for "decoding" the text such as matching words and pictures, and recognising the rhythm of the language in order to predict what comes next. Soon they will start to take on the role of an independent reader, handling and looking at books even if they can't yet read the words.

Most important of all, children should realize that books are a source of pleasure. This stems from your reading sessions which are times of mutual enjoyment and shared experience. It is then that children find the key to becoming real readers.

First published in 1997
This edition published 1999
by Franklin Watts
96 Leonard Street
London EC2A 4XD

Franklin Watts Australia
14 Mars Road
Lane Cove
NSW 2066

Text and illustrations copyright
© Mick Manning and
Brita Granström 1997

Series editor: Paula Borton
Art director: Robert Walster
Photography Steve Shott
With thanks to Ben Ridley-
Johnson.

A CIP catalogue record for this book
is available from the British Library.

ISBN 0 7496 2852 9 (hbk)
ISBN 0 7496 3495 2 (pbk)

Dewey Classification 551.5

Printed in Belgium

Consultant advice: Sue Robson and Alison Kelly, Senior Lecturers in Education,
Faculty of Education, Early Childhood Centre, Roehampton Institute, London.

For Mark – MM

For Gabriel – BG